THE GREAT FARTY SLOB BEAST

Written by Charlie Farley

Illustrated by Joe Barleymow

For Nell – C.F.

For Mardin – J.B.

This edition published by Wacky Bee Books in 2015

Wacky Bee Books
Shakespeare House
168 Lavender Hill
London SW11 5TG
www.wackybeebooks.com

Production by Head & Heart Publishing Services

Title font by Nigel Babb

British Library Cataloguing in Publication Data: a catalogue record for this
book is available from the British Library.

ISBN 978-0-9931109-6-2

Printed in Czech Republic by PB Print

THE GREAT FARTY SLOB BEAST

Written by Charlie Farley

Illustrated by Joe Barleymow

One slovenly, slumbering, midsummer day,
We three had run out of games
we could play.

So being the oldest I said **I'd protest,**

And went to find grown-ups

and tried my **most** best.

'We've played princesses, pirates and tea parties too,
We've played dancing and prancing and hullabaloo.

And now we are bored,' I said, 'Sure as can be,'
While my two little sisters hid right behind me.

'Not now Molly dear,
I'm doing my hair.

Try Father if he's not
a bad-headed bear.'

'Bored!' shouted Father from inside his pit.

'Bored do you say? No, I just won't have it.

Bored is for brats, who are spoiled, who are bad,

Bored children get monsters to play with, not Dad.'

Then we all saw him,

gigantic and hairy,

Smelly and scruffy

and really quite scary.

'I've eaten your dad, and he did not taste good.
That was for starters,
now I'll eat you for pud.'

He scooped us all up – Amy, Lola and Me.

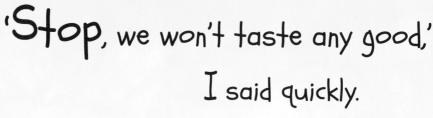

'You'll be breakfast, washed down
with peppermint tea.'

Amy laughed, Lola squeaked, I pretended to cry.
Then thought, I'm no baby like Lola, not I.

'Stop, we won't taste any good,'
I said quickly.

'We'll taste bitter and yucky
and really quite sickly.'

'For kids to taste yummy,
they need to be happy.
Bored kids, it's well known,
taste like Lola's full nappy.

Now, if you would take us
all out for a trip,

To London in one giant hop and a skip,
And show us some sights
and have us some fun,

We're bound to taste nice
when we land in your tum.'

With me on a shoulder,
    Amy under an arm,
For Lola a pocket where she'd do no harm,

Us and the Slob Beast,
    to London we strode.

First stop London Eye,
    on the big wheel we rode.

We sat up on top, little Lola and me.

While Amy and Slob Beast stomp-stomped 1-2-3.

Ker-crash! Went the big wheel,

we scooted away.

To the Aquarium (where I had to pay).

Slob Beast broke the glass and flooded the floors.

Skate, plaice and shark burst out through the doors.

How they swooshed and they slipped, all a-slither and quiver,

Until **Beast**, me and Amy
put them **all** in the **river**.

Amy laughed, Lola squealed
I tried not to have fun,

As I knew we'd end up
in Beast's **bulging** tum.

Next stop, the Palace to peek at the Queen,

Who waved from her carriage all shiny and clean.

Beast muttered to Amy, 'My tummy is grumbling'.

She pulled him away but the grumbling rumbling

went

And **disgusted** the Queen in her carriage.

We **ran away** giggling.

She shouted, 'You savage!'

Where we danced, guzzled **cookies** and raspberry pop.

Then home in a bounce,
Mum had finished her hair,
But didn't look up from her book in her chair.

'I suppose we'll taste good now,'
I said looking sad.

'We weren't bored at all –
I suppose you'll be glad.'

Slob Beast put us down,
        Lola, Amy and Me,
'You know, I'm just too
        tired to eat any tea.'

Off he clomped, and he smiled
        as he went up to bed.

'Maybe, tomorrow,
I'll eat you instead.'